My First Book of Shapes

Circle

A circle is the shape of the sun, a baseball, a pink balloon and a hamster's wheel.

Circles

How many circle do you see?

square

A square is the shape of the window, the **TV**, comfy couch pillows and a birthday gift.

Squares

How many squares do you see?

Rectangle

A rectangle is the shape of mom's cell phone, the refrigerator, a chocolate bar and the door.

Rectangles

How many rectangles do you see?

Oval

An oval is the shape of a mirror, a lemon, an egg and a football.

Oval

How many ovals do you see?

Rhombus

A rhombus is the shape of a kite, a traffic sign and the pattern on the dog's sweater.

Rhombuses

How many rhombuses do you see?

Triangle

FOOTBALL

A triangle is the shape of a slice of pizza or watermelon, nacho chips and a pennant.

Triangle

How many triangles do you see?

Star

A star is the shape of a cookie with sprinkles, a starfish and the topper for the Christmas tree.

Star

How many stars do you see?

Heart

LOVE YOU

I ♡ You

A heart is the shape of Valentine's candy, sunglasses and I love you.

Heart

How many hearts do you see?

Pentagon

A Pentagon is the shape on the soccer ball, a school crossing sign and a house.

Pentagon

How many pentagons do you see?

Octagon

An octagon is the shape of a stop sign!

Octagon

How many octagons do you see?

Hexagon

A hexagon is the shape of a honeycomb and a nut that goes on a bolt.

Hexagon

How many hexagons do you see?

Trapezoid

A trapezoid is the shape of a lamp shade, a flower pot and a bucket.

Trapezoid

How many trapezoids do you see?

Shapes

How many shapes do you see?